Something to Crow About

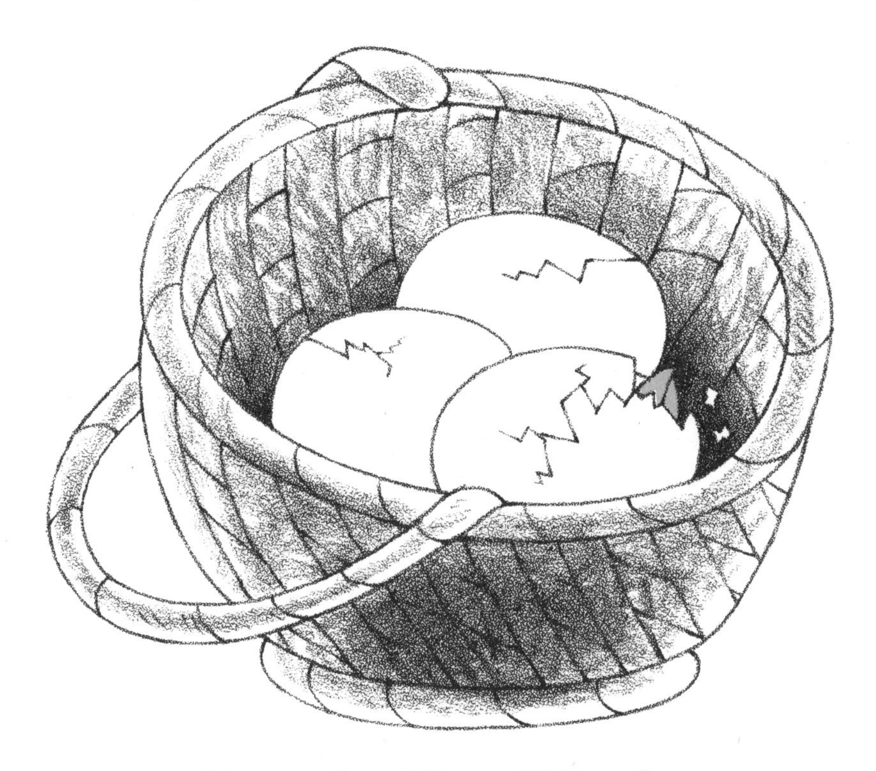

Dorothy Van Woerkom
***Pictures by* Paul Harvey**

ALBERT WHITMAN & COMPANY, NILES, ILLINOIS

Library of Congress Cataloging in Publication Data

Van Woerkom, Dorothy.
Something to crow about.

Summary: When Ralph, a bachelor rooster, finds three orphan eggs on his porch, he decides to brave the trials of single parenthood.

[1. Roosters—Fiction. 2. Chickens—Fiction. 3. Single-parent family—Fiction] I. Harvey, Paul, 1926- ill. II. Title.
PZ7.V39So [Fic] 81-24011
ISBN 0-8075-7534-8 (lib. bdg.) AACR2

The text of this book is set in sixteen point Times Roman.

Published simultaneously in Canada by General Publishing, Limited, Toronto.

For Edith and B.J. Pekich

Ralph was an early bird. He earned his living by waking up his neighbors every morning. He would crow at sunrise, and after that he had the whole day to himself. It was a good life!

One morning just before sunrise, Ralph opened his window and stuck out his head to crow.

COCK-A-DOODLE-DO. . .
AWWKKK!

There, on Ralph's porch, was a basket with three little eggs in it. Ralph flew downstairs and opened his front door.

The eggs were still warm! He brought them into the kitchen and telephoned his friend Harriet. Ralph waited while Harriet's phone rang eleven times.

"Yawn?" said Harriet at last.

"Eggs, Harriet!" Ralph screeched into the phone. "Eggs on my doorstep, in a little basket! What shall I do, Harriet?"

Harriet yawned again. "Eggs?" she said sleepily. "Be sure to keep them warm, Ralph. Are you sitting on them now?"

"*Sitting* on them?" Ralph yelled.

"Or," said Harriet, "you could take them over to the Hatchery. They will find someone to adopt the poor things."

"Good thinking, Harriet," Ralph said. "Thanks."

Ralph hung up the phone. He looked at the eggs. Baby chicks lived inside those white shells. "No, not the Hatchery," Ralph decided. So he spread out his feathers, climbed onto the basket, and sat gently down on the eggs.

By noontime Ralph was hungry. "How do you eat while you are hatching eggs?" he asked himself.

Harriet knew. She came by on her lunch hour with hot corn on the cob. "I was sure you would be sitting on those eggs, Ralph," she said. "I will come back later and bring your dinner."

"Thanks, Harriet," Ralph said. "And Harriet—do you think you could crow for me in the morning?"

Harriet stared at him with her mouth open. "Well, why not?" she said.

Harriet went back to work. Ralph could hear her crowing to herself as she walked away.

"She needs lots of practice," Ralph told the eggs.

That night Ralph could not sleep. His back hurt. His legs were stiff. He was still awake when the sun came up.

"BRRAA-WWWAAAKKK!"

"That was pretty good, Harriet," Ralph said.

Just then he heard a small sound. Something was happening! He jumped off the basket. One of the eggs was cracked. And the other eggs were cracking!

Ralph ran to the phone and dialed Harriet. "I have done it!" he crowed. "I have hatched out two girls and a boy. Now what do I do?"

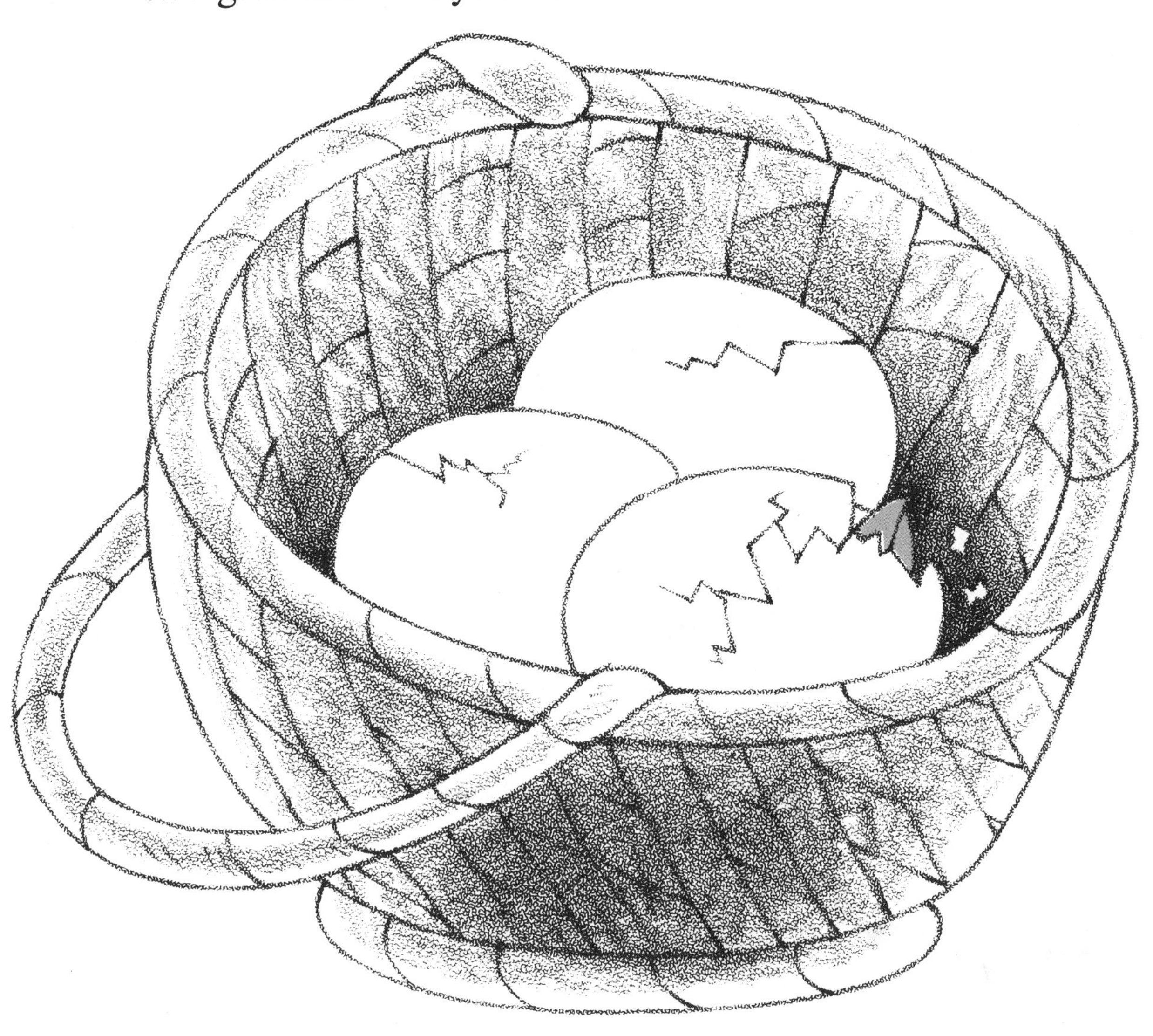

Something told Ralph that Harriet had gone back to sleep after she had crowed in the sunrise. She sounded far away. She mumbled into the phone.

"Mush," Ralph thought she said.

"What, Harriet?" he said. "Speak up."

"I said give them cornmeal mush seven times a day." Harriet hung up the phone.

Ralph got busy and cooked some cornmeal mush. “Why stop and cook up this stuff seven times a day?” he asked. “I will just do up a whole panful at once.”

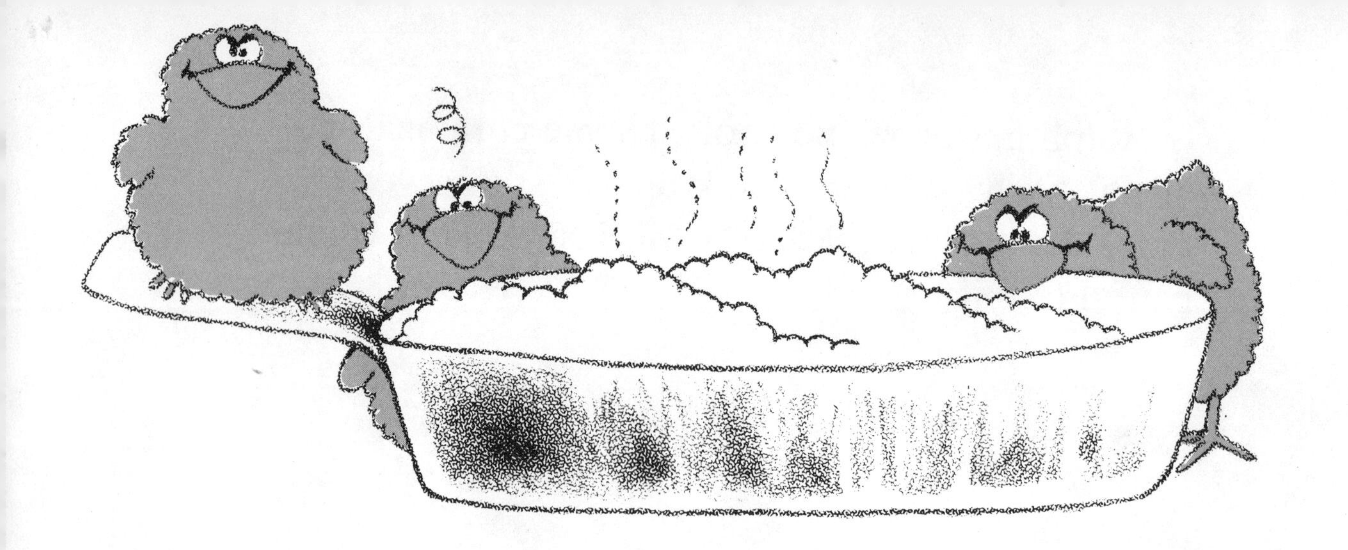

The chicks ate their mush and went back to sleep. When they woke up again, Ralph gave them some more.

Cold! Gooey! Stiff! The chicks would not eat it. Ralph put the mush back on the stove and warmed it.

Hot! Gooey! Stiff! The chicks would not eat it. Ralph sighed. He got busy and made some more.

Delicious! The chicks ate it all up. Ralph ate the gooey stuff himself.

When evening came, the chicks were full of mush and wide awake. They wanted to play. "Not now," said Ralph. "This is bedtime." He brought them upstairs in their basket.

The chicks cheeped and cheeped. Ralph could not shush them. All night long he walked the floor with them. They fell asleep in Ralph's bed just as the sun came up.

Ralph tiptoed to the window and crowed softly, so as not to wake them.

Cock-a-doodle-dooo!

It was not one of his best crows, but it woke the chicks. He shushed them back to sleep and crawled into bed. He closed his eyes.

The telephone rang and the chicks began cheeping again.

"Your crow sounded tired," Harriet said into the phone. "How are things going?"

"Not good," Ralph said. "I can't shush these chicks. I can mush them all day, but I can't shush them at night."

"Put them on the phone," Harriet said.

Ralph put the chicks on the phone. He could hear Harriet's loud, clear voice.

"Your papa will be as mad as a wet hen if you don't stop that," Harriet squawked. "Now, not another peep out of you!"

The chicks shut their beaks and closed their eyes. "Thank you, Harriet," Ralph said.

"Any time," said Harriet.

Ralph named the chicks Arabelle, Sarabelle, and Paul. In no time at all they were old enough to go to school in the Little Red Coop.

The first thing Arabelle learned was how to dance.

"That will be good for her," Harriet said when Ralph told her. "I thought Arabelle was getting pigeon-toed."

Paul was learning to draw. Ralph showed Harriet the pictures. "Have you ever seen such beautiful chicken scratching?" he asked.

Sarabelle took up singing. Harriet clucked. "I wish she would learn something else. She sounds too much like a canary."

One day the chicks came home from school with strange red spots on their beaks and their legs. Ralph looked under their feathers and found more red spots. He telephoned Harriet at her office.

"Chicken pox," Harriet said at once. "Keep the house dark, Ralph. Give them hot corn syrup. I will be right over."

Harriet came and she stayed until midnight. Then Ralph sat up all night watching the chicks. He dozed a little. When he woke up, he saw a bright light shining through the window.

Sunrise! Ralph jumped up. He stuck his head out the window and crowed.

The phone rang. It was Harriet. She said, "Ralph, it is only four o'clock in the morning. You have just crowed for that new light in the supermarket parking lot."

Wearily Ralph hung up. He sat down and closed his eyes. The phone rang again.

"Get some sleep," Harriet said. "When the sun comes up, I will crow for you."

Finally the chicks got well. Ralph told them, "Tomorrow is your Aunt Harriet's birthday. I think we should do something special for her."

"Let's have a picnic," said Paul.

"With corndogs and popcorn!" Arabelle said.

"I will sing Aunt Harriet the birthday song," said Sarabelle. She began to practice.

Ralph threw up his wings and rolled his eyes. Sarabelle still sang like a canary.

"While Sarabelle is singing," Ralph said to Arabelle, "you and I will plan the picnic."

"I will make Aunt Harriet a birthday card," Paul said.

It was a wonderful birthday picnic. Ralph and Harriet watched the chicks playing ball.

"What dears they are," said Harriet fondly. "Just look at Paul. He is already growing a lovely red comb!"

Ralph's chest feathers puffed up with pride. "They really are something to crow about," he said. "Thanks for all the help, Harriet. I could never have done it all so well without you."

Harriet was eating a corndog. "Braawwk," she said with her mouth full.

But Ralph knew what she meant. Just being around while the chicks grew up was thanks enough for Harriet!